AUSTRALIAN SEALIFE

Mason Crest Publishers
www.masoncrest.com
Philadelphia

Mason Crest Publishers
370 Reed Road
Broomall, PA 19008
(866) MCP-BOOK (toll free)

Copyright © 2003 by Mason Crest Publishers.

All rights reserved. No part of this publication may be reproduced or transmitted in any form or by any means, electronic or mechanical, including photocopying, recording, taping, or any information storage and retrieval system, without permission in writing from the publisher.

First printing

ISBN 1-59084-211-1

Library of Congress Cataloging-in-Publication Data on file at the Library of Congress

First published by Steve Parish Publishing Pty Ltd
PO Box 1058, Archerfield BC
Queensland 4108, Australia
© Copyright Steve Parish Publishing Pty Ltd

Photography by Steve Parish, with
    p. 6: Hans & Judy Beste
    p. 8: Mark Simmons
    pp. 14-15: Darryl Torkler (The Photo Library, Sydney)

Printed in Jordan

Writing, editing, design, and production by Steve Parish Publishing Pty Ltd, Australia

CONTENTS

Sea life of Australia	5
Penguins	6
Whales	9
Dolphins	10
Sea turtles	13
Sharks and rays	15
Reef fish	16
Bannerfish	18
Angelfish	21
Clownfish	22
Wrasses	25
Cleaner fish	26
Trevally	29
Moray eels	32
Fish with venom	34
Dangerous animals	36
Mollusks	38
Camouflage	40
Crabs and crays	42
Sea stars	45
Hard and soft coral	46
Sponges	48
Worms	49
Index of animals pictured	50
Further reading and internet resources	51

Use of Capital Letters for Animal Names in this book
An animal's official common name begins with a capital letter.
Otherwise the name begins with a lowercase letter.

3

SEA LIFE OF AUSTRALIA

Australia is surrounded by sea. In the salt water and on the shores live fascinating creatures. Some are easy to find. Others hide under rocks, in the sand, and deep in the water.

The first animals you might see are seabirds flying in the sky.

At the beach there are crabs and mollusks. In reefs and out in the open sea are fish, corals, and many other animals. Some are harmless to humans, but some can be dangerous.

Australia's seas are filled with interesting creatures to discover.

▲ The Salmon Holes, Western Australia
◄ The Great Barrier Reef

▲ A Great Barrier Reef island

PENGUINS

Penguins live in the cool waters of the southern oceans. They cannot fly, and their wings have become more like flippers for swimming. Their webbed feet also help them to swim fast.

Penguins have short, thick, waterproof feathers that keep them warm and dry. A layer of fat underneath their skin also keeps them warm in the cool sea water.

The Little Penguin is also called a "fairy penguin." It is the only penguin that breeds in Australia. Between August and February, these penguins can be seen parading along the southern beaches at dusk.

▲ A parade of Little Penguins.

Little Penguin ▶

WHALES

▲ Humpback Whale flipper

Humpback Whales feed in the cold sea around Antarctica all summer. In winter, they swim to warmer waters around Australia.

Some female whales have babies after reaching the waters off the Northern Australian coast.

They feed their babies milk, but do not eat anything themselves until they have gone back to the cold southern oceans.

A male whale leaps into the air to show off to a female he hopes is ready to mate with him.

◀ Male Humpback Whale

DOLPHINS

Dolphins are not fish. Like whales, they are mammals. They have warm blood and feed their babies milk. Their arms have become flippers, and their tails beat up and down, not sideways, like fish tails.

When a dolphin wants to find out about something, it sends out sounds that bounce off the object and back to the dolphin. The dolphin's brain can then make a mental picture from the echoes. This is called sonar.

▲ Bottlenose Dolphin and baby.

Bottlenose Dolphin ▶

▲ Green Turtle swimming.

SEA TURTLES

When a female turtle is ready to have babies, she crawls up the beach and digs a big hole in the sand. She lays a lot of soft-shelled white eggs in the nest. Then she fills in the hole, leaving her eggs there. The baby turtles hatch and run down to the sea. They will have to survive many dangers before they grow up.

▲ Baby turtle hatching.

▲ Green Turtle laying her eggs.

13

SHARKS AND RAYS

Sharks and rays are fishes, but they do not have bones. Their skeletons are made of soft gristle, like at the end of your nose, called cartilage. Sharks are hunters with sharp teeth. The huge Manta Ray is harmless to humans. It feeds on tiny animals called plankton.

◀ Whaler Shark

Manta Rays ▲

REEF FISH

The fish that swim around a coral reef are often brightly colored and patterned. Some brightly colored fish become darker or duller at night when they go to sleep. This change in color could be to protect them from their enemies.

A female fish may have different colors from a male. Some types of fish can change sex. This can happen as the fish grows older or to keep the numbers of males and females balanced. If a fish changes sex, it will also change colors.

▲ Coral Trout

Squirrelfish and Regal Angelfish ▶

BANNERFISH

Bannerfish live in pools of warm, clear water around coral. They eat tiny animals they find on the coral. Like many coral fish, bannerfish have bright colors and markings.

During the day, bannerfish dart among the coral. At night, they tuck themselves into safe places to sleep. While they sleep, their colors and markings fade so enemies cannot find them.

▲ Masked Bannerfish

Longfin Bannerfish ▶

ANGELFISH

A family group of adult angelfish guards their part of a coral pool. They want to keep the food on the coral for themselves. They chase away other adult angelfish, but may allow young angelfish to stay. This is because young angelfish have different colors and patterns from the adults. These markings show that the young fish are not a threat to the adult group.

◀ Emperor Angelfish

Half-Circled Angelfish ▲

CLOWNFISH

Clownfish live among the poisonous tentacles of sea anemones. To do this safely, clownfish have found a way of tricking the anemones. First, the clownfish finds an anemone it wants to live in. It brushes past the tentacles many times, becoming covered with the anemone's jelly. Then the anemone does not harm it.

▲ Pink Clownfish

Orange-Fin Clownfish ▶

WRASSES

Wrasses are a group of brightly colored fish. The Harlequin Tuskfish, which has blue teeth and stripes of red, green, and blue, belongs to the wrasse group. The Thick-Lipped Wrasse in the picture below is sucking in sand. It eats the tiny animals living in the sand, then puffs the sand back out into the water again.

◂ Harlequin Tuskfish

Thick-Lipped Wrasse feeding. ▴

CLEANER FISH

Fish carry small animal and plant pests between their scales. Fish in a group called cleaners nip these pests away and eat them. A cleaner fish will wait at a "cleaning station." By swimming in a special way, it tells other fish that it is ready to clean them. When a fish comes to the station, the cleaner fish swims all around it, even into its open mouth, cleaning off its pests.

▲ Cleaner fish and Coral Trout

Cleaner fish and Coral Cod ▶

TREVALLY

Groups of ocean fish, like trevally, live in deeper water. The scales of a trevally are shiny and silver, like mirrors. This makes the fish hard to see when they swim near the surface of the water. Trevally are fast swimmers and travel together in large groups called schools. A school of trevally looks like one big fish as it changes direction.

◀ Gold-Spotted Trevally   A school of Golden Trevally. ▲

MORAY EELS

Moray Eels spend the day in holes and under the ledges of underwater rocks. At night, they come out and hunt fish, crabs, and crays. Their sense of smell is keen, and their teeth are very sharp. However, they are not dangerous to humans.

To breathe, eels take in water through their mouths and send it over their gills. The gills take oxygen from the water.

▲ Moray Eel

Two Moray Eels ▶

Fish with Venom

Some fish are dangerous. The bright stripes of the Lionfish warn other animals not to touch it, for its back fins are tipped with poison. The Stonefish looks like a weed-covered rock as it lies on the bottom of a pool. It also has venom on its back fins that can harm someone who steps on it.

▲ Stonefish   Lionfish ▶

DANGEROUS ANIMALS

▲ Sea jelly

Many sea creatures can be dangerous. Sea snakes have fangs that inject venom. Sea jellies have tentacles with tiny poison stings. The Blue-Ringed Octopus has a sharp beak and a venomous bite. A sea urchin's spines can break off and stick in an animal's flesh.

▲ Olive Sea Snake

▲ Blue-Ringed Octopus   Ijima's Sea Urchin ▶

MOLLUSCS

Mollusks have soft bodies, often protected by shells. Bivalve mollusks live between two shells. They include oysters, mussels, and clams.

Gastropod mollusks, such as cowries and cones, have one shell. Nudibranchs are mollusks that have no outside shells.

Nautiluses, octopuses, cuttles, and squids all have tentacles. They form a group of mollusks called cephalopods. Octopuses have eight tentacles, but cuttles and squids have eight shorter arms and two longer tentacles.

The empty shells of mollusks often wash up on the beach.

▲ A giant clam is a bivalve.

▲ A nudibranch

▲ A bubble shell

▲ A cone shell

CAMOUFLAGE

An animal may hide from its enemies or hide in ambush, waiting to catch other animals to eat. When an animal hides against a background that has similar coloring or texture, it is said to use camouflage.

Many sea creatures can change their own coloring to match their resting places. Other animals have skin that always looks like their surroundings. They can camouflage themselves just by staying still.

▲ Wobbegong Shark

The octopus can change color. ▶

40

CRABS AND CRAYS

Crabs and crays have soft bodies protected by hard outside skeletons. Crabs and crays have 10 legs. Some of the legs end in claws that are used to pick up food and threaten enemies. Some legs are used for walking. Crabs and crays do not have separate heads to turn, but their eyes are on moveable stalks.

▲ A female crab looking after her eggs.

Painted Cray ▶

SEA STARS

▲ Sea star

Sea stars, brittle stars, and feather stars are related. A sea star has five arms. Underneath its arms are lots of tiny tubes, each ending in a sucker. The sea star uses these suckers to move. Brittle stars have five long arms that break off easily. A feather star has many arms that trap tiny animals to eat.

◀ Feather star   Sea star ▲

Brittle star living on soft coral. ▲

HARD AND SOFT CORAL

Coral animals are called polyps. Each polyp has a soft body with a mouth and tentacles at one end. A polyp of hard coral builds a wall around its soft body. Then it pushes its tentacles out the top to catch its food. A polyp of soft coral does not build a wall. Its body is supported by little pieces of crystal inside it, the same way that our bones hold up our bodies.

▲ Feeding tentacles of polyps of Sunshine Coral

▲ Soft coral

SPONGES

▲ Sponge

The sea sponges sold in shops are the skeletons of dead sea animals. The body of a living sponge covers its skeleton in a thin layer. To feed, a sponge sucks in water through holes in its body. It strains tiny animals out of the water and eats them. Then it pumps the water out again.

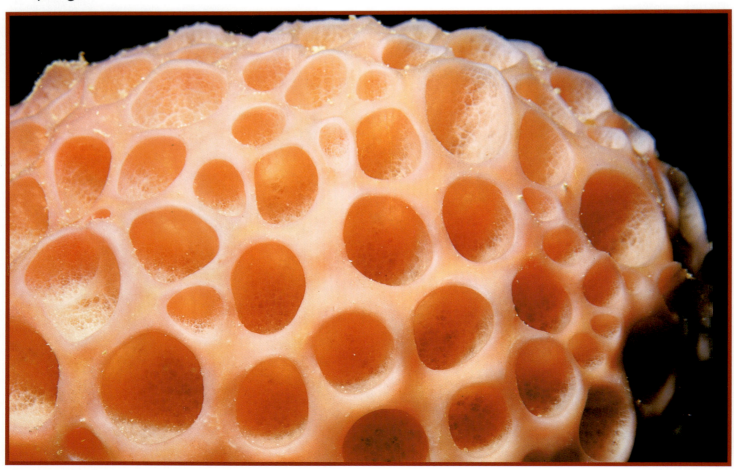
▲ Sponge

48

WORMS

Many kinds of worms live in the sea. Some burrow through the coral or the sand. Some swim freely through the water. Others build themselves tubes from sand or coral.

Feather Duster Worms have crowns that catch tiny plants and animals for the worm to eat.

▲ Feather Duster Worm

▲ Christmas Tree Worm

INDEX OF ANIMALS PICTURED

Angelfish, Emperor, 20
  Half-Circled, 21
  Regal, 17
Bannerfish, Longfin, 19
  Masked, 18
Brittle star, 45
Clam, giant, 38
Cleaner fish, 26, 27
Clownfish, Orange-Fin,
  22 -23
  Pink, 22
Cod, Coral, 27
Coral, soft, 45, 47
  Sunshine, 46
Crab, 42
Cray, Painted, 41
Dolphin, Bottlenose, 10, 11
Eel, Moray, 32, 33
Feather star, 44
Lionfish, 34-35
Nudibranch, 39
Octopus, 41
  Blue-Ringed, 36
Penguin, Little, 6, 7
Polyps, 46
Ray, Manta, 15
Sea jelly, 36

Sea Snake, Olive, 36
Sea star, 45
Sea Urchin, Ijima's, 37
Shark, whaler, 14 -15
  Wobbegong, 40
Shell, bubble, 39
  cone, 39
Sponge, 48
Squirrelfish, 17
Stonefish, 34
Trevally, Gold-Spotted,
  28 -29
  Golden, 29
Trout, Coral, 16, 26
Turtle, 13
  Green, 12, 13
Tuskfish, Harlequin, 24-25
Whale, Humpback, 8, 9
Worm, Feather Duster, 49
  Christmas Tree, 49
Wrasse, Thick-Lipped, 25

FURTHER READING & INTERNET RESOURCES

For more information on Australia's animals, check out the following books and Web sites.

Cerullp, Mary M., Jeffrey L. Rotman (photographer), and Michael Wertz (illustrator). The Truth About Great White Sharks. (April 2000) Chronicle Books; ISBN: 0811824675

The great white shark—quite possibly Australia's most famous marine fish—is also a creature that is largely misunderstood. Learn how to separate the truth from the myths about great whites.

Weir, Bob and Wen Weir. Baru Bay: Australia. (April 1995) Hyperion Press; ISBN: 1562826220

This beautiful picture book teaches readers about the coral reef animals of Australia.

Arnold, Caroline. *Australian Animals.* (August 2000) HarperCollins Juvenile Books; ISBN: 0688167667

Seventeen unusual animals from Australia are introduced in this full-color book, including koalas, possums, gliders, quolls, Tasmanian devils, platypuses, echidnas, kangaroos, wombats, dingoes, snakes, and penguins.

Morpurgo, Michael, Christian Birmingham (illustrator). *Wombat Goes Walkabout.* (April 2000) Candlewick Press; ISBN: 0763611689

As Wombat wanders through the Australian bush in search of his mother, he encounters a variety of creatures demanding to know who he is and what he can do.

http://home.mira.net/~areadman/aussie.htm

This Web site contains a comprehensive listing of the sealife of Australia, with further links to in-depth information on various species.

http://www.nativefish.asn.au/

This site is dedicated to Australia's native freshwater fish and contains information on hundreds of fish (found under Fish Files). It also provides a listing of extensive links to other sites and organizations dedicated to all Australian fish, both saltwater and freshwater (found under Oz Fish Links).

http://www.amonline.net.au/fishes/students/flash/index.htm

Children of all ages will love playing this online Fish Memory Game. After correctly matching a pair of cards picturing a certain Australian fish, players are given brief bits of information about the animal whose picture they just matched.

http://www.wildlife-australia.com/

This Web site is actually for the Chambers Wildlife Rainforest Lodge in Queensland, Australia, but it provides hundreds of links to all sorts of Australian rainforest creatures. From frogs to birds, reptiles to butterflies, if it lives in the Australian rainforests, you'll find in-depth information on it here.

http://rainforest-australia.com/

This other Web site for Chambers Wildlife Rainforest Lodge contains even more extensive information and photos on Australia's rainforest animals. Find information on the different levels of the rainforest environment; see pictures of the various creatures that inhabit each layer; and learn about Australian animals, from dingoes to lizards and everything in between.

NATURE KIDS SERIES

Birdlife
Australia is home to some of the most interesting, colorful, and noisy birds on earth. Discover some of the many different types, including parrots, kingfishers, and owls.

Frogs and Reptiles
Australia has a wide variety of environments, and there is at least one frog or reptile that calls each environment home. Discover the frogs and reptiles living in Australia.

Kangaroos and Wallabies
The kangaroo is one of the most well-known Australian creatures. Learn interesting facts about kangaroos and wallabies, a close cousin.

Marine Fish
The ocean surrounding Australia is home to all sorts of marine fish. Discover their interesting shapes, sizes, and colors, and learn about the different types of habitat in the ocean.

Rainforest Animals
Australia's rainforests are home to a wide range of animals, including snakes, birds, frogs, and wallabies. Discover a few of the creatures that call the rainforests home.

Rare & Endangered Wildlife
Animals all over the world need our help to keep from becoming extinct. Learn about the special creatures in Australia that are in danger of disappearing forever.

Sealife
Australia is surrounded by sea. As a result, there is an amazing variety of life that lives in these waters. Dolphins, crabs, reef fish, and eels are just a few of the animals highlighted in this book.

Wildlife
Australia is known for its unique creatures, such as the kangaroo and the koala. Read about these and other special creatures that call Australia home.